I CAN HELP

AF228194
Rourke
Educational Media
A Division of
Carson Dellosa
Education
MARLA CONN

Photo Glossary

baby

books

chairs

cooking

groceries

trash

I can help with the **baby**.

baby

I can help with the **books.**

I can help with the **chairs**.

I can help with the **cooking.**

11

I can help with the **trash.**

I can help with the **groceries**.

groceries

1. Go back to the story with a reading partner. Discuss how the children are helpful.

2. Brainstorm ways we can be helpful in our home community and school community.

3. Why is it important for people in a community to help each other?

4. Use your ideas to make a chart on a separate sheet of paper.

Ways we can help at home	Ways we can help at school

5. Draw a picture showing how you are helpful at home and at school.